The Emperor's New Clothes

Illustrated by Mike Gordon

Retold by Susanna Davidson
Based on a story by Hans Christian Andersen

Once upon a time there was an
Emperor who loved clothes.

He liked looking splendid
ALL the time.

He had a different outfit for every day of the year.

But the Emperor had a problem.
He had nothing to wear for
the royal procession.

"Won't any of your outfits do,
Your Highness?" asked
his servant, Boris.

"NO!" said the Emperor. "I need a
NEW outfit and I need one NOW."

"And remember – it has to be
splendid."

Boris sighed and set off to find the finest clothes-makers in town.

WANTED!
Splendid new outfit for the Emperor. Clothes-makers apply here!

NO TIME-WASTERS PLEASE

He wasn't having much luck until...

a little round man

and a long thin man
rushed up to him.

They bowed with their
bottoms in the air.
"We are Slimus and
Slick, at your service,"
they said.

Boris took them to the Emperor.

"We make magic clothes," Slimus told him.
"Only clever people can see them. Stupid people can't!"

"Are they splendid?" asked the Emperor.
"Very splendid," promised Slick. "But very expensive.
We'll need pots and pots of money."

"Take all the money you want," cried the Emperor.
"Just make me those clothes!"

A week later, the Emperor and Boris went to see Slimus and Slick at work. "Welcome!" they said. "What do you think of our clothes?"

The Emperor gulped. Boris gulped.
Neither of them could see a thing.

But they didn't want to look stupid.
So the Emperor said, "Splendid!"
"Yes, really very... splendid," said Boris.

"Oh, um, er, most splendid!" added the footmen.

Here! Have more money.

As soon as everyone
had gone, Slimus
and Slick laughed
and laughed
until their faces
turned purple.

Then they ordered a huge feast.
"It's hungry work making magic clothes," they said.

On the morning of the
royal procession, the Emperor
couldn't wait to put on his new clothes.

"Here is your cloak," said Slimus.
"It's light as a feather."

"Oh Your Highness," said Slick. "You look
very handsome. Your clothes fit so well."

The Emperor admired himself in the mirror. "Don't I look splendid?"

"Yes, Your Highness," gasped the footmen, staring straight at the Emperor.

"Yes, Your Highness," said Boris, staring straight at the ceiling. (He was trying NOT to look.)

"Open the palace gates!" ordered the Emperor. "Let the royal procession begin."

The crowd gasped
when they saw the Emperor.
Everyone had heard that only clever
people could see his clothes.

"Aren't his clothes splendid?" they said.

"Let me see him!" called a small boy, who was stuck at the back of the crowd.

"Ooh!" said the boy. "The Emperor's got no clothes on!"

Faster than a spreading fire,
a whisper whizzed
through the crowd.

The Emperor heard their words. He looked down.
"Oh no," he thought. "I'm naked!"

Then he blushed
bright red.

"But I can't stop now. This is the royal procession and I am the Emperor."
So he held his head high and walked on.

The crowd clapped and cheered. They thought it was the most splendid royal procession ever!

Edited by Jenny Tyler and Lesley Sims

Cover design by Russell Punter